THE LORD OF THE CRYSTAL

A MYSTERIOUS CALLING . . .

PREETI PRABHAS

Contents

About The Author

Preeti Prabhas, the author of 'The Lord of the Crystal, A Mysterious Calling...' is a fascinating storyteller and an enthusiastic educator of English Language and Literature, who shares a splendid relationship with learners. She weaves magnetic tales which trickle down gently into the reader's hearts, leaving them yearning for more. She evokes dynamic characters to walk out from the pages of history, adorning the role of protective guardians, reminding of what they owe. Born in West Bengal to Keralite parents, she was brought up with her siblings in the heartland of India, Gwalior, that stands tall with its majestic fortress, temples, and palaces – a testament to its glory. She is the recipient of the Inspirational Guru Award 2022, from the eminent author Shri Chetan Bhagat, at the Transforming India Conclave held at Sree Saraswathi Vidya Mandir, Mettupalayam, Tamil Nadu. She was honoured on Teachers' Day 2022, by the esteemed Member of Parliament, Shri. Hibi Eden, at Bhavan's Munshi Vidyashram, Kerala. Her interests include reading, nature exploration, and yoga. She loves to hear from readers. Feel free to contact her on the mail id- authorpreetiprabhas@gmail.com

Instagram- preetiprabhas

LinkedIn- linkedin.com/in/preeti-prabhas-educator

Facebook- Preeti Prabhas

Acknowledgements

The Lord of the Crystal is the most precious creation, amongst all my innovative writing explorations. The journey from its inception to culmination was supported by an array of well-meaning hearts who illuminated the path and kept the spark of inspiration glowing.

I am indebted to the almighty for guiding me through thick and thin, empowering me to manoeuvre and accomplish the task, day in and day out.

My parents nourished me with beautiful thoughts, teaching me to rise when I fell and believing in myself. I thank my parents for enriching me with the gift of education besides the unconditional love that they shower on me.

My sister, Reeti, nephew, Achintya, and my son, Tanish were a true blessing, as their curiosities added flair to my creativity.

My joy knew no bounds when a set of enthusiastic and innovative teenagers assisted in shaping the cover design idea, envisioned by me. I truly appreciate the efforts of my nephews, Achintya, Aagneya, and my son, Tanish. Thank you, my dears for shaping my dreams.

I am truly touched by the magnificent ways in which my well-wishers have brightened my day. Your support means more to me than words can convey. I feel blessed to have such amazing people in my life.

I acknowledge sincere gratitude to my teachers who polished my innate skills and lit my path. I bow to the wisdom and godliness in everyone around me.

Dear reader, I am overwhelmed by the seamless love that you have showered on me, your priceless feedback,

ACKNOWLEDGEMENTS

reviews, and the time that you have invested, traversing through 'The Lord of the Crystal.' Your support inspires and motivates me to create more enchanting stories.

Preeti Prabhas

Note From The Author

Dear Readers,

Greetings!

I am delighted to share with you a few interesting moments from the journey of penning down this special piece of fiction. I would love to believe that it must have been the call of destiny which could have compelled me to strive through pressing times, letting my pen travel through the unknown path, portraying fresh ideas, and keeping the flame of curiosity blazing.

Though it was a solo creative venture, it kept me charged throughout – infusing life into imaginative characters and giving them the power to defend the weak and vanquish the evil; letting them pick thorns that bled the hearts of their loved ones – boldly facing fiery trials – thriving on the timeless virtues of love, trust, and loyalty.

I hope, you find reading it as rewarding an experience, as I felt while instilling the characters with their specific traits, laughing with them in their joy and shedding tears in their distress. When they felt trapped, I wielded the power of my pen to save them. That is when I wondered, 'Is this how God feels, when we call for help, and he becomes our saviour?'

'The Lord of the Crystal, A Mysterious Calling . . .' is absolutely dedicated to creating happy swings in paradise for you and your loved ones – away from the bustling crowd.

Happy Reading!

Loving regards,

Preeti Prabhas

CHAPTER ONE

It was a hazy morning. Thick fog draped the streets of Pune, endlessly, like a blanket of white spray over the stubborn rays of sunlight that strived to find its way through the smoky canvas.

If a dream is worth it, chase it; blessings will follow, Trisha mused, unaware that what passed her mind as a casual thought, would soon unfurl as an eventful journey, shrouded in mystery.

A gentle breeze blew a wave of golden-brown hair across her face as she strolled on the terrace of her office which was her usual way of giving a fresh start to a hectic day.

Trisha's long straight-line sea-green kurta paired with greenish yellow slim-fit pants complimented her fair skin. Her twin-shaded chiffon chunari gleaming with sequin seemed to strike sweet musical notes on the strings of the rhythmic breeze that mischievously swayed past her feminine charms.

Hearing quick footsteps, she turned around curiously. Her beautiful chocolate brown eyes settled on the tall dusky figure facing her with a sparkle in his eyes and a sweet crescent curve adorning his lips, exuding an unassuming charm.

'What are you doing here, Trisha?' Neel asked.

He was Trisha's colleague, who had joined Dream Dales as a 3-D designer, about six monthsago. He was amiable and had a knack of making people smile and laugh with his light-hearted approach.

'Just came out to enjoy the fresh breeze. The fog hasn't settled yet,' Trisha replied with a smile.

After graduation, Trisha had joined the firm as an Interior Designer, a year ago. Her extraordinary aesthetic sense could transform any earthly space into heaven.

'Happy birthday to you!' Neel wished her, extending a red rose towards her which he had been hiding behind him till then.

'Oh! Thank you so much! How did you come to know it is my birthday?' she asked, her countenance blossoming into a bright smile. A red rose was the least she had expected as a gift from Neel. She was puzzled as she wondered why he chose a rose above everything else.

'Why don't you come down?' he asked.

'Oh sure! I was about to . . . but the pleasant weather held me back.'

'I think you are needed for something important; others were searching for you.'

'Let's go,' Trisha said.

Without a second's delay, she walked down swiftly, and Neel followed.

'This is the perfect place for this rose, else it will droop down by the evening,' Trisha said, turning towards Neel, as she slid the rose in the flower vase, placed near the staircase.

It was decked with lively, pleasant orchids and roses. She caught a glimpse of disappointment flickering across his face. She did not intend to hurt his feelings, but she wished to keep the gift a secret from her colleagues, just to escape their naughty questions. She knew how they would pounce upon such topics, for sheer fun.

As they reached the entrance of their office, the glass door slid open. Stepping into their designing space was like entering a marvellous world where sophistication met the classic splendour of nature. Huge glass windows rising from the floor to the ceiling, usually allowed different hues of sunlight to shimmer across the mahogany flooring, throughout the day, but that day, due to fog, sunlight entered the hall sparingly, so the glowing interior lights took charge of lighting up the place). The off-white netted curtains added to the ambience of the grand hall.

The ceiling of the high rising hall glowed with a variety of illuminations.

Sleek models of tables and cushioned chairs in earthy shades complimented the colour theme of the infrastructure, providing the designers with their individual space, as well as freedom for collaborative discussions.

Towards the left side of the entrance, a tall circular revolving bookcase, stood majestically, decked with a variety of world-class inspirational design books. It attracted ample attention from inmates to blend and develop their ideas, to match various lifestyle choices.

Soft cushioned couches and sofas found their place in the right corner of the hall, with a beautifully carved glass teapoy in the centre. This area was designed for discussions with clients. The presence of ornamental plants created an inviting environ, contributing to a feeling of tranquillity to handle tough situations with ease.

A light invigorating music played in the backdrop to keep the mind calm and focused. A subtle citrus scent floated in the air.

When Trisha and Neel entered, everyone burst out, showering birthday wishes with smiles and laughter. A velvet birthday cake with her name embossed on it was displayed grandly on the table. It was indeed a pleasant surprise for her. Soon Trisha cut the cake and a fresh day began on a happy note.

That evening, the delivery boy entered with packets of snacks which Trisha had ordered for her colleagues.

'Are there more surprises in stock, Trisha?' Jay asked jovially.

Trisha responded with a cheerful thumbs up, which seemed to convey, 'Wait and watch!'

Jay was one among those lucky guys who had turned his passion for 3-D modelling into a profession.

'Please join in guys and gals,' Trisha said, inviting her colleagues for the treat.

'Help yourself with burgers and litchi juice,' Sim, the receptionist, at Dream Dales, seconded Trisha's invite exuberantly.

As everyone settled with their share of delicacies and chilled sweet drinks, they started clamouring for songs.

Trisha's fascination for melodies was an open secret, just as her stunning designing skills were. Neel suggested one of the latest hit numbers. Trisha was quick in humming the tune.

Neel stepped forward with a bewitching smile and said, 'Come on, join me for the song.'

He struck the note:
'Oh, my darling damsel!
There is none like you,
A million worlds around.
When you tire of walking alone,
Call me once,
I will be right beside.'
Trisha picked the notes:

'Heh!
I walk this world,
I call mine!
And heard many -
Who call me amazing,
And dream a walk -
Beside me.'
Neel:
'Oh, my darling damsel!
The world may change,
Just as seasons do,
Trust my heart,
It beats for you.'
Trisha:
'I flutter around . . .
With swaying satin robes,
Don't put it on me,
If your heart's lost . . .'

As Neel and Trisha took the lead, others joined in with snaps and claps and rhythmic thumping of fingertips, on the tables. Smiles and laughter floated in the air and the clock seemed to tick faster than its usual pace. It struck six and it was time to wind up. They had stayed an extra hour for the celebrations. Gradually, everyone parted with sweet goodbyes.

As Trisha reached the staircase, she did not forget to pick the rose from the flower vase. Neel, who was walking ahead of her, chanced to turn back, and saw her carefully tucking the flower in her bag. As she looked up, she saw Neel smiling at her. She passed an embarrassed smile at him and walked with quick steps to join others who were on the way down the stairs.

When she reached home, her father asked her anxiously, 'What happened Baby Doll? Why are you so late today?'

Baby Doll was her nickname; her father called her so, lovingly.

'Sorry dad, I should have informed you. I gave a treat to my colleagues today,' she said.

Her father's anxieties melted, and it gave way to a pleasant smile. They walked together to their living room where her mother and her siblings were waiting for her to commence her birthday celebration.

CHAPTER TWO

Sunday mornings, Trisha and her younger sister, Swish took charge of the breakfast preparation. That day, they prepared khaman dhokla, a savoury cake. It was their favourite Gujarati dish, made of Bengal gram flour.

Daze, her younger brother, was swinging and swaying to the musical beats of the trending songs. Mom helped him with the dhokla. His face lit up when he took the first bite; his expressive beautiful eyes widened with joy, and it went without saying that the dish was delicious. He was the first one to be served food in the family. That was the norm. He was the darling of the family.

That Sunday, everyone in the family agreed that the breakfast was yummy. They savoured every bit of it.

When Daze was just six months old, crawling, and chasing his ball under a glass table that was placed in the centre of their living room, something horrifying and unexpected happened. The glass top crumbled down to pieces and fell all over Daze. The edge of the glass flower vase, kept on the table, hit Daze's head before crashing on the floor and breaking into innumerable pieces. Blood started oozing from his head. Trisha picked up the yelling baby. Swish ran to call mom and when she reached the scene, she was shocked to see Daze bleeding and screaming with pain. Mom felt as if her energy was draining off. She took him in her arms carefully, trying to calm him with her warmth and her caring words, as she motioned to ring up dad. Swish picked up the phone with a trembling hand and rang up her father, but the call could not be placed. Desperately she rang the next number. It was Uncle Josh's number who was their neighbour. He was quick to respond. In the next couple of minutes, his car steered to a halt at the gate. Without wasting a moment, they ushered mom and Daze into the car and Trisha accompanied them to the hospital.

The moment dad got the news from Trisha, he left all his work in the office and was beside them.

Doctors were able to save him, but his brain suffered irreparable damage. Daze took nearly two months to recover.

The mishap occurred when Trisha was just twelve and Swish was all of ten.

From that day on, Daze developed a phobia, and he would not step down from his bed without support. He would tremble whenever he had to walk a few steps. He needed assistance to do all his tasks.

Everyone took extra care of Daze, trying to keep him happy always. He loved music. His favourite pastime was listening and watching songs on television. That made him happy.

Gradually, Daze became the centre of everyone's love and attention. He was innocent and cute. He would control everyone from his bed with his adorable remarks. If anyone got angry and spoke in a high tone, he would say, 'Cool, cool.' Heights of temper could be easily mellowed into smiles and laughter by his timely responses. His innocent comments were based on his close observations of all that happened in his surroundings. Though he could not speak with clarity, a careful listener could easily understand what he meant.

He had to miss normal school due to his handicap, but he joined a special school.

As time rolled by, everyone picked up threads of hope in expectation of happier days.

Ten years had passed, since the tragedy struck their lives. On every holiday, they would make sure to spend time together. Mom, dad, Swish and Trisha enjoyed chit chatting about the news in the morning newspaper or the news channels. They updated each other about the recent happenings in and around the family and even incidents beyond their immediate circle.

'Did you hear about the recent incident in the neighbourhood?' A young man was caught drawing symbols on the boundary wall of Mr. Seth, the businessman, who lives in the opposite lane,' said mom.

'Oh! When did all this happen?' Swish enquired with concern. Trisha was curious too.

Mom continued, 'Just yesterday. He was caught and questioned by Jeet, Mr. Seth's son. Riya, his sister, identified him as her classmate and revealed that the youth had been stalking her for a week or so. Somehow, he managed to get her contact number and rang her at wee hours, but as she was not interested, she blocked his number. He drew unfathomable symbols, taking inspiration from the gang of robbers who left similar symbols on the wall as a warning sign, a few days before the actual robbery. This was a desperate step taken by the young man to grab her attention.

Trisha shook her head in disapproval and asked with a frown, 'Did the police arrest him?'

'Yes, he is under police custody now,' dad replied.

'Girls, be careful of such guys. Avoid taking lifts from strangers. There are so many cases of kidnapping, and we cannot predict anyone's true colours until and unless we know them well,' mom added with concern.

'Oh mama! Do you think we are so naive? We are not kids anymore,' Swish, a second year Humanities student, responded with a smile.

'Don't worry mom, we will take care,' Trisha said, trying to brush away her mom's concern.

Concern for her daughters was clear on mom's face as she walked towards the lawn to water the plants.

CHAPTER THREE

Diwali celebrations were around the corner. Everyone in the office had planned a get together on Choti Diwali, the day prior to Diwali, the festival of lights.

That morning, Trisha walked towards her first-floor office, wearing a crimson lehenga and a multi-coloured choli, lighting up the corridor with dancing reflections from its glass embroidery. Her chiffon chunari, with streaks of greenish blue, hung from her shoulder, its other half trailing behind her, complementing her attire. Traditional silver accessories added to her charm. Sparkling droplets hung at the tip of her thin danglers that swayed with every step that she took. A part of her straight glistening hair graced her shoulders while the rest drooped down behind her, till her waist.

A beautiful dream catcher adorned the corridor, just before the entrance. The glass door to her office slid open and Trisha entered. A romantic number played in the backdrop.

Neel was seated on the couch, near the door, adjusting some decorative frills.

Sim and Jay seemed busy, checking something on the laptop, perhaps selecting songs for the party, Trisha assumed. They were facing the opposite direction of the door, at the far end of the hall, unaware of Trisha's entry.

Neel waved at Trisha. She looked stunningly beautiful, nothing less than a diva. She waved back at him pleasantly, but quite unexpectedly, she slipped, and was about to fall, when a strong grip on her waist, held her midway. Instantly, she opened her eyes and was shocked to realise that she was settled on Neel's lap. He held her in his arms, pulling her tightly towards him, reassuring her safety. For a moment, they were speechless, not knowing what to say. Embarrassed, Trisha tried to regain her posture, as the awareness of her surroundings dawned on her. Hesitantly, she raised her right hand, and placed it on Neel's shoulder to get back on her feet.

'Take it easy!' said Neel gently with a smile and gradually released his tight hold around her.

Trisha blushed, but tried to smile and managed to say, 'Thanks Neel.'

She heaved a sigh of relief when she looked around and saw no one except Jay and Sim, who were engrossed with their work. The music was loud, and she was glad the awkwardness of the situation went unnoticed.

She quickly adjusted her hair and attire, while Neel's admiring eyes struggled to look away from her.

He said, his lips curved in a half smile, 'You are nothing less than lightning today!'

'Oh, really!' Trisha responded with a quick shy glance at Neel, meeting his adoring gaze.

'You look dashing, too,' Trisha commented, running her eyes over him, head to toe, observing how handsome he looked in the heavily embroidered, front buttoned, knee-length white kurta paired with slim-fit pyjamas.

'Let's decorate the place together,' Neel said.

'Yeah sure, I'll be right back after meeting Jay and Sim,' Trisha replied, and she walked past him swiftly, holding up her lehenga, a little off the floor, to avoid tripping.

'Hi Sim, Happy Diwali!' Trisha greeted.

'Hi pretty girl, Happy Diwali!' Sim responded with a twinkle in her eyes.

'You look lovely too!' Trisha cooed gleefully, holding Sim's hand, and observing her, who wore a chiffon baby pink saree with a beaded matching blouse and jewellery.

'Did you get all the songs that we had listed?' Trisha asked.

'Yeah! Apart from the ones that we chose, Jay added a few more festive music collections to it,' Sim replied.

'Wow! Trisha, you look awesome,' Jay commented, diverting his attention from the laptop, and extending his arm for a handshake.

Trisha smiled infectiously and waved her hand playfully, avoiding a handshake, as she greeted him, 'Happy Diwali, Jay. You look handsome too . . .'

Her voice almost trailed off as she observed Jay's palm, which had been extended for a handshake, now locked in the strong grip of an arm whose owner stood behind her. Trisha turned around and was surprised to see Neel with an envious smile and piercing gaze, settled on Jay.

'Save your handshake for your sisters, Jay,' he taunted.

Jay returned an icy stare, as he freed himself from his opponent's iron hold. Then a naughty expression lit up his face as he spoke, settling his silky hair with a stroke of his fingers, 'Hi dude!'

'You forgot to shake hands with me . . . or . . . is it that you shake hands with pretty girls only?' Neel teased Jay.

'Oh! Sorry that I missed out on the chronological order for shaking hands,' retorted Jay, expressing his amusement.

Before the interaction could continue, there was a hustle-bustle, as other colleagues started pouring in with loud laughter and Diwali greetings. Everyone looked cheerful.

Neel raised his brows and looked at Trisha, as if to ask what her plans were.

'I'll join you for decorations,' Trisha replied.

She turned towards Sim and asked, 'What are you planning to do next?'

'I am waiting for the flowers which Nia had promised to deliver for the floral rangoli.

'Why hasn't it arrived yet?' Sim voiced her concern looking impatiently towards the door. I got a message from Blooms, the flower store, about two hours ago that it had been dispatched. I hope it reaches here soon. I can help with decorations, till the flower boxes arrive,' Sim added.

'Yeah sure!' Trisha responded, turning towards Neel for agreement.

Neel smiled warmly and said, 'Come on, join in.'

He held out packets of multi-coloured wall hangings to the two young ladies and they proceeded with the task of decoration.

Sim looked inquiringly towards Neel and asked, 'Weren't you a little harsh with Jay, today?'

Trisha turned towards Neel and remarked, 'He is such a sweet guy.'

'Sweet guy! Eh? Hmm . . . I was just kidding. Don't take it too seriously,' Neel grinned and alighted from the stool where he had perched himself for setting up the decorations.

Sim looked at Neel with a know-all kind of mischievous smile and then shifted her focus towards Trisha, who was studying Neel with narrowed eyes.

'I will get some welcome drinks for both of you,' Neel said, trying to escape the embarrassing situation.

'What do you prefer: strawberry, pineapple, or cashew-almond shake?' he asked.

'Cashew-almond for me,' Trisha voted.

'Strawberry shake,' Sim voiced. Neel walked towards the counter where fruit shakes were being served.

'He diverted the discussion smartly,' Sim said.

Trisha nodded, studying her funny expression, and added, 'Yeah. I think he was just being jovial, but it went a little too far. They are basically good friends. Hopefully, things would smoothen out between them, soon.'

By then, Neel joined them with three glasses of fresh fruit shakes on a tray. Trisha noticed that there were two glasses of cashew-almond.

As they enjoyed sipping the shake, a young man entered with a carton in his hand. Sim identified him as the flower delivery boy.

'Please leave it on the table,' Sim said to him pointing to the receptionist's table.

'Ladies and gentlemen, your attention please,' Sim announced. 'The flowers for the floral rangoli have arrived. The talented, young ladies and gentlemen who are interested can join in.' All heads turned in her direction.

'Sure, we are there for rangoli,' a few colleagues voted.

'I'll be with the team of petal pluckers,' Neel and Trisha declared almost together.

'I am with the team, too,' Sim and Jay hummed in, followed by Harsh.

Harsh, the Head of the Human Resource Department at Dream Dales oversaw the party that day.

Jay knelt with a pack of coloured chalk to draw the pattern on the floor. He was quick at finishing it.

Soon, all the members of the team settled down to pluck petals for the creation of floral designs. Trisha was soon ready with yellow dahlia petals. Kneeling beside her, Neel contributed orange shades from marigolds. Sim handed over the white corolla of daisies while Harsh offered hues of blue and lavender. Soon, an amazing floral rangoli took shape. All of them clicked snaps gleefully around it and made sure to flash it on social media.

A buffet was arranged for lunch on the terrace. After enjoying a sumptuous meal, some chose sweet drinks while others relished fruit ice-creams. Trisha picked a sweet yoghurt drink with a thick fresh cream topping while Neel joined her with a blueberry ice cream cone.

Suddenly the music stopped, and Harsh announced from the stage. 'Ladies and gentlemen, we are going to begin a couple dance in a short while. There are two separate bowls for ladies and gentlemen, containing names of participants on folded slips of paper. We will pick a slip randomly from each bowl. The selected couple will have to perform on the ongoing music.' Sim joined Harsh to announce the names of the couples as they had volunteered to anchor the event.

Lively couple dances began, and the participants entertained the gathering. They tapped their feet and swayed to the tune of an array of enticing romantic numbers. Trisha's heartbeat rose as she waited for her turn.

'Trisha and Jay,' the names were announced. As they proceeded to the stage, the names of the upcoming participants were announced too.

'Neel and Trisha,' the announcers, seemed puzzled, as to how Trisha's name appeared twice, as only one slip per person had been dropped in the bowl. They were sure, somebody had played a prank.

As confusion pervaded, Harsh came up with a solution. 'It's up to Trisha to decide whom she wants to pair up with.'

'As you say, I have no hitches. I can dance with both of them,' replied Trisha sportively, standing halfway up the stairs to the stage.

'Oh great! You made our task easier. So, you can change your partner when the music pauses. If you agree, we can continue,' said Harsh.

'Yes, I'm ready,' Trisha replied with a thumbs up.

The music started, 'Fiza . . .' There was a loud uproar as Trisha ascended the stage along with Jay. All their colleagues started clapping to the tune, as they held each other's hands and swayed to the tune of the romantic number. Suddenly the music paused and within seconds Neel was on stage. Jay stepped down.

The music struck again, and Neel held out his arm. Trisha swung with him gracefully. Every step that they took, set the floor ablaze. Among the onlookers, Harsh, Sim and Jay snapped and clapped, encouraging them with smiles of appreciation. After the dance, Trisha and Neel stepped down.

'Fantastic!' Sim remarked, smiling cheek to cheek. She ran towards them and shook hands with Trisha and Neel simultaneously, her eyes full of admiration.

Harsh announced, 'That was a sizzling performance by Neel and Trisha.' Other colleagues followed suit and almost everyone surrounded them, with words of appreciation.

'What a wonderful dancer you are, Trisha!' Neel said, beaming with delight. 'I'm glad we were paired together,' he continued, breathing heavily.

'Too good to believe, you were an amazing partner too, Neel!' Trisha echoed almost in chorus with Neel. We made it, she said, gushing with laughter. Joy spilled from their hearts as they smiled and laughed.

'But the question remains, who could have dropped my name twice?' Trisha wondered aloud, loud enough for Neel to hear.

'If it is neither of us then it could only be Jay. Anyway, don't rack your brain about such trivial matters. Aren't you happy with the outcome?' Neel asked, trying to leave a happy trail.

'Yeah true,' Trisha agreed with a smile.

She continued, 'Can we get something to drink?'

'Sure, we will go for some rejuvenating citrus drinks,' Neel said, and they walked towards the counter.

They settled down for some time with their fizzy lemonades.

Soon Harsh announced, 'Today's dance performances were a treat to the eye and an ecstasy to the soul. As we draw to the close of this sizzling event, it is time to begin today's most auspicious ceremony of lights. Shortly, we will gather on the terrace for aarti to evoke Goddess Lakshmi and seek divine blessings for happiness and prosperity.'

A mellow music continued to play, as the audience gradually ascended the stairs.

Trisha lit her first earthen lamp, immediately after aarti. Sim joined her. They started arranging the lamps on the terrace wall. When Trisha turned around to pick the next lamp, she stood face to face with Neel whose smiling face gleamed in the light of a dozen lamps, which he held, arranged on a platter in a circular fashion.

'You are just in time. We finished arranging our lot,' Trisha said.

Her glance shifted from Neel to his companion. It was Jay, smiling warmly, holding a bottle of oil to refill the lamps, which had drained out.

'Where did you vanish, Jay? I didn't know that you are so good at dancing,' Trisha gushed.

'You were graceful too,' Jay commented with a twinkle in his eyes.

'Tell me, frankly, wasn't it you, who had dropped an extra name slip with my name on it?'

Jay grinned and replied, 'Yeah! I had a bet with Neel that I would dance with you today.'

'Is it so Neel?' Trisha asked.

Studying his expression of ignorance about the whole episode, she commented, 'So that is the reason why you were so sure that it could only be him.'

Neel grinned and shrugged his shoulders.

'There's more to it, Neel's bet was that if anyone danced with you today, it would be only him.'

'Oh, this is news . . .' Trisha said, with wide eyes and open palms, expressing surprise.

Neel looked at Jay with narrowed eyes and asked, 'Whatever said and done, don't you agree that it was real fun?'

'Oh really?' Trisha said, looking at Neel and Jay with an amused look on her face.

Soon the terrace was shimmering with flickering lights, as everyone joined in to decorate the whole place with lighted lamps.

The dusky sky had taken a beautiful crimson hue. Sunlight gradually started fading, with the night setting in.

'Oh! I am getting late. It is already 6:30. I need to rush back home. I'll change my lehenga and be back in a moment,' Trisha said, almost in a single breath.

'What is the hurry? Wouldn't you have dinner?' Sim's voice dropped short, as Trisha was already halfway downstairs. Within seconds, she changed her attire and was back in the company of her friends.

Soon, she returned wearing a pink boat neck top and sky-blue jeans. This makeover from traditional to modern, suited her well.

'Sorry friends, I can't wait for dinner. You see, it is my dad's rule that we should be home by 6 p.m. I am leaving. Bye . . .' Trisha waved.

Jay and Sim waved too.

'Wait a second. I will walk you down,' Neel called out to her, as she hurried down. He tried to keep pace with her.

Soon they reached the parking lot.

'By the way, why do you always follow me?' Trisha asked Neel, looking at him with a side glance.

'What do you think?' Neel asked a counter question.

'Don't throw the ball back into my court,' Trisha said.

'The parking area is deserted, so two is always better than one. And isn't it a friend's duty to see off another friend?' Neel's question was his reply too.

Trisha stopped midway, turning towards him, searching for truth in his eyes. Neel grounded himself too, facing her. He was not smiling. He gazed at her for a moment seriously, his eyes as deep and fathomless as the ocean.

'We will talk later. Aren't you getting late?' Neel asked.

'Tonight, I'm going out of town,' he said after a moment's silence.

'Where are you going, and why such a sudden trip?' asked Trisha curiously.

'To visit my uncle. My cousins have been inviting me over for quite some time, so I promised to celebrate Diwali with them,' Neel said.

'Enjoy your trip,' Trisha said with a smile, digging her hand into her bag, and searching for her key.

'What do you like the most?' Neel asked, watching Trisha fumbling with her bag.

'Why are you asking that now?' Trisha asked, delving out the key.

'You'll get to know soon,' Neel said.

'Sometimes you are very secretive, if only I could read your thoughts,' Trisha said playfully.

'Don't think too much, it's not rocket science,' Neel grinned.

Trisha walked a few paces towards her two-wheeler, then turned back facing Neel and replied with a slight smile, 'Lotus.'

Trisha nodded as she started her vehicle and waved.

Neel waved back with a smile.

That night after dinner, Trisha was reclining on a pillow, on her bed, reading a memoir.

Swish was already asleep. She slept early that night. A light music was playing on the stereo which was gifted to her by her father on her fifteenth birthday.

Suddenly Trisha's mind wandered to Neel.

'Where could he be now? What could he be doing? Must be travelling,' she thought.

Why was he so interested in her? Was it only friendship or something deeper than that? What did he want to say? He lingered in her thoughts for some time. She tried to bring herself back to her reading. She felt restless, wanting to know what Neel felt for her. She closed the book and kept it under her pillow.

She glanced at the statue of Krishna, the ever-smiling Lord, in the inbuilt case on the wall, specially designed for showcasing artefacts. Krishna was her best friend from her childhood. She found him extremely charming, so she had placed the statue of the Lord in her room, as he infused in her, a feeling of positivity. Moreover, she felt secure under his protection.

'Do you like Neel?' she asked Krishna. She closed her eyes and envisaged the image of Krishna in her mind, with his flute on his lips. She could visualise a pleasant expression on his face. She knew that it meant, 'Yes.' Whenever she was in a fix, she would turn to her Lord for an answer. If his answer was 'No' his image would flicker.

She was glad, her Lord liked him too. She smiled back at Krishna.

She felt at ease as she settled herself cosily in her muslin quilted blanket and was fast asleep within a few minutes.

CHAPTER FOUR

A strikingly charismatic, unearthly youth with wavy shoulder length hair and enchanting eyes appeared before Trisha, lighting up the surroundings with his radiance. He spoke in a soothing voice with an endearing smile lingering on his lips, 'Go to the Krishna temple in the East and accept the divine crystal that Maharshi Trikaldarshi offers you. It will bestow miraculous powers upon you. I am with you.'

Surprised, Trisha woke up, switched on the light and looked around but couldn't spot anything unusual; everything was intact. She shared the room with Swish who was fast asleep on the bed nearby.

The strange dream left Trisha restless. She decided to visit the temple, the next day itself, as she had an inkling that it was none other than Krishna who had appeared before her a few minutes ago. She looked at the statue of Krishna and asked, 'What do you want me to do, Krishna?'

The night was still, except for the chirping of crickets. She knew something extraordinary was going to happen, and it would be a turning point in her life, as well as, for many others; but she had no clue what destiny had in store for her.

The morning of the grand festival, Diwali, dawned. The moment Trisha woke, the divinely gracious figure of her dream flashed across her memory and his deep voice rang in her heart. Trisha took a shower and was soon ready to go to the temple.

Swish looked at her with sleepy, blinking eyes and asked, 'Where are you going so early?'

'I am going to the temple.'

'What's the time now?' Swish asked with a perplexed look on her face.'

'It's 4 AM,' replied Trisha, clipping her wet hair. She wore a sky-blue straight cut, long kurta with white Luchnowi chikankari embroidery, paired with moderately loose white pants and a soft, white embroidered chiffon chunari.

'Happy Diwali, Swish!' Trisha's early morning wish was filled with enthusiasm.

'Happy Diwali!' replied Swish, in a quavering tone, as the speciality of the day struck her, though her half open eyes were still weighed down by sleep.

'I would have joined you if you had chosen to go a little later,' Swish continued.

'That's fine, I'll go alone,' saying so, Trisha smiled and walked out into the garden with a netted flower basket. It was made of artistically inter-twined, glazed cane strings – a beautiful piece of art, which she had picked from an inter-state trade fair while on a visit to her aunt's place. She plucked jasmines, red roses, royal blue butterfly pea flowers and basil leaves till her basket was full, to be taken to the temple as an offering to the Lord.

'I'm going to the Krishna temple, Maa,' Trisha informed her mother in a hushed voice, as everyone else in the family was asleep. Her mother was getting ready to recite her daily morning hymns.

'Keep a torch handy, and go carefully, Trisha,' she said, as it was pitch dark outside. The streetlights lit the pathway to the temple, but the torch was an additional safety measure.

The Krishna temple was just a few kilometres away, and visiting the temple early in the morning was a norm for devotees.

Trisha reached the outer premises of the temple and walked towards the huge wooden entrance with intricate carvings on either side. Then she bent and touched the stepping stone with devotion before setting foot into the inner compound. Treading the stone pavement, she reached the inner main entrance from where she crossed a dimly lit pathway flanked by hanging oil lamps on either side, till she reached a wide space surrounding the sanctum. Many more devotees had assembled there, for the early morning rituals. She could see the stunning deity clearly, made of black granite inside the sanctum sanctorum – draped in yellow robes, decked with sparkling jewellery, a flute on his smiling lips, and a peacock feather adorning his curly hair. She kept her offerings on the stairs that lead to the Lord. She joined her palms with reverence and closed her eyes in prayer.

After a minute's silent prayer, when she opened her eyes, she was startled to see Gurumata Ritambhara Devi standing beside her, as if waiting to say something. She was dressed in a white saree and a full sleeve white blouse with a slightly raised standing collar. Her right arm held the corner of her saree in a loose grip, wrapping herself completely. The long sandalwood tilak with a speck of sindoor in the centre of her forehead and the basil leaf garland around her neck added to her piety.

Trisha bowed and said, 'Namaste Gurumata!'

'Namaste! Maharshi Trikaldarshi has sent me here to escort you to Chandrashala,' said the graceful *sadhvi*.

Trisha wondered how Maharshi Trikaldarshi knew that she would be visiting the temple that day and, precisely, at that moment. Nevertheless, she followed Gurumata to the hall of learning, where the Maharshi imparted spiritual guidance to seekers trapped in the dark alleys of uncertainty, desperately trying to find solutions to their problems in the materialistic world.

The large hall, supported by huge, beautifully sculpted granite pillars, rang with the chanting of Om, by the disciples who were assembled in the hall on grass mats in meditative posture.

Trisha bowed before the Maharshi, who was seated in padmasana, meditating on the stage, seated on a straw mat. He was clad in a saffron cotton dhoti and a shawl with its one end overlapping the other on his shoulder. His glistening grey eyebrows, moustache, beard, and long twisted hair held in a bun on top of his head, added to his divine aura. Garlands of blueberry beads, popularly known as rudraksha, adorned his bun, neck, and arms. An elongated U-shaped sandalwood tilak graced the centre of his forehead, with its base taking a leaf-like shape on the bridge of his nose, and a smaller, tapering red tilak beautifying its centre.

He gradually opened his eyes, maintaining his calm posture, as if aware of Trisha's presence and said, 'Welcome, I have been waiting for you. I know that the Lord sent you here. He appeared before me while I was in meditation and said that I must hand over his divine crystal to you.'

Trisha was amazed at the stunning coincidence of her dream with the Maharshi's divine vision. Though almost unbelievable, it was true.

The Maharshi said, 'In the next few moments, we will be transported to a divine realm shielded from human reach.'

Saying so, the sage opened a beautifully crafted silver case revealing a soft ivory silk fabric, which unfurled, letting its edges slip down daintily from the case. It unveiled a mesmerising celestial crystal, flanked by lavender mountain ebony flowers, placed on the shining silk fabric in the case.

'This is the most precious and extremely powerful gem, the Will-o'-Wish, infused with infinite energy. It will protect and guide you to vanquish all evil forces. It will remain invisible to everyone, except you,' Maharshi Trikaldarshi disclosed.

'Extend your palm,' the Maharshi instructed gently. Trisha held forth her right palm overlapping the left, with utmost reverence.

The Maharshi uttered a hymn with closed eyes and the sparkling crystal, rose in the air and settled on her palm, infusing a powerful transformation within her which was beyond expression.

'Never reveal to anyone that you are in possession of the divine crystal and refrain from using it for personal gains,' the Maharshi commanded.

Trisha bowed in obedience. She accepted the sandalwood paste which the Maharshi offered and applied a slight vertical streak in the centre of her forehead. Then she took leave from him and sought

the blessings of the Lord before retracing her steps towards the temple exit.

Something uncanny was about to unfurl– but what and how? she wondered. She knew, the Lord always had a strong purpose behind his manifestations, which would eventually lead to a larger good. So, she decided to wait for the right moment to get a convincing answer to her inquisitiveness. She rode back home, unassumingly, preparing herself mentally for her new animated role, which she would have to play, soon.

Once back home, Trisha's thoughts went back to her childhood days when she and Swish would help their mother with all the festive arrangements and preparation of delicacies. On one such occasion, she had asked her mother innocently, 'Why is Diwali so special, maa?'

Her mother had answered lovingly, 'When Shri Ram, the beloved crown prince of Ayodhya returned to his kingdom after a long exile of fourteen years, his subjects welcomed him by lighting lamps all over the city. That memorable day is celebrated every year by the people as Diwali, the festival of lights.'

Trisha joined her mother and Swish in the kitchen to prepare malpua, a special sweet made from milk.

'Trisha, keep stirring the milk frequently, otherwise, it would stick at the bottom of the pan,' mother warned.

'Swish, slice the dry fruits to be sprinkled on the sweet dish,' she continued.

Soon, the sweet dish was ready, and everything was set for the celebrations.

In the evening, all family members assembled in the living room, dressed up in the best of their attires for the puja. As per the custom, Trisha's mother offered the delicacy, which they had prepared, to the presiding deities – Shri Ganapati, Shri Ram, Mata Sita, Lakshman, and Goddess Lakshmi. Soon after the puja, she distributed the offerings among the family members.

Everyone contributed to the decoration of the entire house with lighted earthen lamps, especially the terrace, the staircase, the lawn, and the boundary walls. They made sure that every nook and corner of the house was well-lit. In addition, dad's arrangements: decorating the trees, windows and doors with shimmering lights gave a dazzling effect to their house, even from a distance, as it stood out among the brightly lit neighbourhood. The town was bedecked with the lights of the lamps which equalled the enthusiasm in the hearts of the jovial men, women, and children.

Trisha and Swish burst crackers, while others in the family had fun watching the fire-show. Daze sat on a chair and enjoyed the activities. Fresh snaps of the family celebrations soon graced the social media pages.

CHAPTER FIVE

The next morning, in the office as Trisha was working on a new design, the intercom rang.

'Trisha, please come in.' It was Mr. Cruz, her boss, who was an occasional visitor to the office, as most of the time he would be on official tours across India and abroad.

'Good morning,' Mr. Cruz, Trisha greeted him with a smile as she entered his cabin. Mr. Cruz met almost everyone with a lively spirit and positive attitude. The respect that he gave, always earned mutual respect, not just in the form of valuable relationships, but also, it paved the path for advancements in his career by building trust and positive professional connections.

'Good morning,' came a pleasant reply from her boss.

He ushered her to take a seat opposite to him across the glass table. She made herself comfortable on the seat, which had a round cushioned base and well-padded arm and back support.

'We have an ambitious project coming up, designing the interiors of a college campus. This time you, Aanchal, Neel, and Jay will handle the project.'

'Sure, Mr. Cruz,' replied Trisha with enthusiasm.

'Today, Aanchal is on leave, and Neel will join after half-day. We will soon arrange a meeting with all four of you, so that we can move ahead with the project, as soon as possible,' Mr. Cruz said.

'Who will lead the project?' asked Trisha curiously, with an anxious note.

'Is something bothering you? You can speak to me frankly,' Mr. Cruz continued.

'When Aanchal and I worked together on the last project, she asked me to hand over all my designs to her, as she didn't have enough time to go through them here in the office and I did so, as I was subordinate to her, but shockingly, she presented my designs as her own.'

'Oh, I see!' Mr. Cruz narrowed his eyes and added, 'This time you both can send your designs to my mail directly. The one who presents the best designs would lead the project.'

'Thank you for considering me for this project,' Trisha said pleasantly as she came out of the cabin.

Later in the day, she was busy working when she felt someone bending onto her table. Startled, she looked up. Resting his elbow on the table, Neel looked at her with smiling eyes, 'What's up?' he asked with a raised eyebrow.

'You almost scared me. Take a seat, there's news for you,' Trisha smiled.

'Did you miss me?' he asked, looking at her intently for a moment, then his lips broke into a quizzical smile.

Though amused, Trisha tried to maintain her gravity, and said, 'Be serious sometimes Neel; I have to talk to you about something official.'

'Oh! Then let us be official,' saying so, he pulled a chair and sat down.

'Mr. Cruz called me this morning and said that we are going to work on a new project. You, Aanchal, Jay, and I will be part of it.'

'Interesting!' Neel said.

'But I have some apprehensions working with Aanchal because of my past unpleasant experience,' Trisha said.

'I too felt that she was a shady character. Then, what did you do?' Neel asked with concern.

'I discussed the matter with Mr. Cruz,' Trisha said.

'Right! It is better to raise your voice against such exploitation, rather than tolerating it,' Neel said, seconding her stand.

Trisha nodded. 'By the way, I forgot to ask you about your trip,' she said casually.

'It was great fun, as I met my cousins after a gap of nearly six months.'

'Nice to hear that. Did you have lunch?' she inquired, as it was time for lunch.

'Yes. What have you brought?' Neel asked, shifting his attention back from his colleagues who were moving out to the cafeteria for lunch.

'Fried rice and kadai paneer,' Trisha replied.

'Would you like to join me for lunch?' she asked.

'Sure, I can give you company, though I'm full,' Neel said as they walked towards the cafeteria.

They took seats and Trisha opened her lunch box. Offering it to Neel, she said, 'You wouldn't surely mind having some.'

Neel took the first bite and exclaimed, 'Wow, this is yummy! Who prepared it?'

'My mom!' Trisha said pleasantly.

'I wish aunty would invite me to lunch someday.'

'Why not? She would be glad to meet you,' Trisha added with a smile.

Neel could not take his eyes off, Trisha's radiant smile. He liked the way her lips curved, when she smiled.

'Keep smiling and laughing, always. You have a ravishing smile. Didn't anyone tell you before?' he asked.

Trisha waved her hand across her face smilingly and dismissed the topic lightly.

Back at the office after lunch, Neel pulled out a paper bag from the shelf and held it out to Trisha.

She looked at it with amazement and asked, 'What is it?'

'Open it and see for yourself,' Neel said, slightly tilting his head with eagerness to watch Trisha's expression as she opened the bag.

She could hardly believe her eyes when she pulled out a beautiful lotus bud from its cover.

'Oh, how sweet! Where did you get it from?' she asked with a bright smile.

'On our way back, we drove past a lake and saw these beautiful flowers in blossom.'

'I'm so glad that you brought it, but how could you pluck a lotus? Doesn't it grow in muddy water?' Trisha asked curiously, her eyes twinkling with joy.

'When I stepped into the water, I realised that my foot was sinking. Somehow, I could reach this one.' Neel said.

'Why did you take so much trouble?' Trisha asked.

'To see this smile on your face,' Neel replied with a smile of satisfaction gradually brightening his face.

'Oh! How I wish it would never lose its freshness. This would beautify my living room. Thank you, Neel, for presenting this marvellous gift.'

'Have you ever been in love?' Neel asked suddenly.

'Not really,' replied Trisha, pursing her lips, and shaking her head, with surprise evident in her eyes. 'What about you?' she continued.

Neel looked away from her for a moment then fixed his glance on her.

'Hmm . . . to be frank, I had a crush in my high school days. She was my classmate, Netra, but I could never muster the courage to express my feelings for her,' he said as if recollecting those days.

'She is one of our family acquaintances, too,' he added.

Trisha liked his honest answer, as well as his gesture of going out of his way, just to see a smile on her face. Nobody had ever made her feel so happy. No one ever cared to fulfil her wishes, except her parents.

But she was unable to understand him completely. 'Was he still in love with Netra? If so, why was he so concerned about her happiness?' her thoughts wandered. Finally, she decided to leave it to herself.

'Hey! Where are you? . . . Lost in thought?' Neel asked, snapping his fingers.

Trisha fluttered her eyes as she came back to the moment with a jerk and replied with a smile, 'No, nothing.' She felt embarrassed and wondered if he had read her thoughts.

'Let's get back to work,' she said, pulling out a file from her drawer which contained the details of the new project.

Neel observed her for a moment, then said, 'Ok, as you say, work first.'

The day passed. It was a busy one, as usual.

Later, when she reached home, she slid the long stem of the Lotus bud in a flower vase, half filled with water, and placed it at the centre of the teapoy in her living room, as she had promised.

'Oh wow! Where did you get such a pretty lotus from?' Swish asked her.

'One of my colleagues brought it,' she replied jovially and proceeded to freshen up, humming a tune to herself.

CHAPTER SIX

'I have seen your designs. Well done, Trisha! They are simply exquisite. You will lead our new project, *D'light D'signz*. It should be a true source of delight for our clients,' said Mr. Cruz in a short meeting, held with all four members of the team.

'Thanks for the opportunity,' Trisha said, while Jay and Neel smiled and nodded. Stupefied, Aanchal refrained from expressing her feelings.

Once out of the cabin, Aanchal said, 'Mr. Cruz will realise soon that he has made a serious mistake by choosing a novice to lead the project.'

It all happened on a Friday, and the next Monday morning Mr. Cruz called for an urgent meeting with Trisha.

He said, 'Aanchal has submitted her resignation citing personal reasons. So, we need to appoint an interior designer. Join me for the interview to select the new candidate.'

'Sure, I'll be there,' she nodded. As she came out of Mr. Cruz's cabin she thought, 'Could there be an ulterior motive behind Aanchal's hasty resignation?'

That night Trisha had a strange dream. A gorgeous lady emerged from a dark stormy cloud. Drifting towards her, she whispered, like a hissing serpent, 'Come with me to the Land of Happiness.'

Though she was attractive, there was something insensitive about her. Sinister vibes emanated from her, and her eyes wore an icy sparkle. Her hair with a frosty sheen lashed like a surging wave - rising and falling, as she rode the storm cloud.

The next moment, the vision was overtaken by a bold echoing voice-

'Beware of her!
She loots happiness,
Drowning the people in despair.'
'Unveil her vicious plans!
Awaken the youth,
And crush her empire!
Summon the Will-o'-Wish!
To dispel darkness.'

Trisha woke up with a shudder and saw a dazzling crimson lightemanating from the Will-o'-Wish. The deep voice which woke her up was familiar. It was none other than the Lord himself who was guiding her on the path of karma.

She knew, it was time to expect the unexpected. She decided to face the odds, come what may.

She looked out of the window and saw streaks of light, gleaming through the branches of towering trees. She smiled, welcoming the dawn -*the dawn of awakening.*

She folded her quilt and spread her bedsheet. After a shower, Trisha settled herself on a mat and recited the hymns which she chanted every day for divine protection and guidance. Then, she continued with her regime of yoga and meditation.

That day, Trisha joined Mr. Cruz to conduct an interview for the selection of a new interior designer for the firm.

Suddenly the crystal on Trisha's palm started glimmering with a crimson hue. It was a warning signal that made her even more vigilant. Just then, the third candidate entered the cabin. Trisha was shocked to see the mystery woman - the lady with the dark energy, who had barged into her dream, inviting her to the Land of Happiness. Her profile said, she was a freelance interior designer. Anybody who crossed paths with her would invariably glance at her, at least twice, such was her bewitching persona.

The clash between light and darkness was closing in; it would begin any moment, sooner than Trisha had expected. Her first strategy was to stay alert and refrain from divulging any secrets of the firm in the presence of her opponent. She decided to observe all her moves till the right moment arrived to unravel Goonj's actual identity.

After an exchange of greetings, Mr. Cruz said to Goonj, 'Please take a seat.'

Once she settled herself on the opposite seat, he continued, 'Introduce yourself.'

'I am Goonj, the go-getter. I don't wait for opportunities to come my way, rather I grab them.'

'What are your achievements?' Trisha asked.

'I have been in the field of interior designing for a period of six years and I have worked on six projects. Each design of mine was a show stealer and an instant success with my clients.Now, my ambition is to prove my mettle on larger projects,' Goonj's confidence, bordering on arrogance, spilled from every word that she uttered.

Mr. Cruz seemed impressed.

'Please share the location of your previous projects,' Trisha said.

Goonj shifted her attention from Mr. Cruz to Trisha, her piercing glance fixed on her for a moment.

'Yes, it would be great to get a glimpse of your achievements,' Mr. Cruz added with a smile.

The brightness on Goonj's face seemed to fade, as she stirred a little uncomfortably, then replied, 'Sure, I will share it with you as early as possible.'

'You can take a seat in the lounge until we call you,' Mr. Cruz said. Goonj was led by the office assistant to the waiting area adjacent to Mr. Cruz's office.

'Thank you,' Goonj said as she rose and walked out of the cabin.

'What's your opinion about Goonj?' Mr. Cruz asked Trisha.

'I feel she is overconfident. She can do us more harm than good,' Trisha said.

'Why do you feel so?' he asked.

'My sixth sense says so,' Trisha replied.

'If you can prove your point, I'll agree with you,' Mr. Cruz said.

He seemed to have taken a special liking for her and had almost selected her for the role. Trisha knew, it was difficult to convince him.

'Please give me a day's time before we finalise the candidate. I will update the details about Goonj at the earliest,' Trisha said.

'I feel it is difficult to get such a competent candidate, so instead of rejecting her outright, let her join today for a trial period of one week. You all can get to know each other by that time,' Mr. Cruz said.

If Trisha was given a choice, she would never have allowed Goonj to join their firm. She decided to move ahead cautiously, till she could unravel the mystery that shrouded the newcomer.

Trisha was not surprised when Goonj accepted Mr. Cruz's offer to join the office immediately.

A pretty and fashionable lady walked with an airy gait into their large office space, where all the staff members were seated, immersed in their work. Suddenly, dark clouds rumbled, the weather darkened, and thunderbolt struck. The electricity tripped, automatically shifting to the alternate source, the solar power.

Goonj, dressed in a figure-hugging white shirt and sky-blue stretch jeans waved, passing a lovely smile at everyone in the office. Remnants of a red free-flowing jacket clung to her shoulders, the rest of it seemed to follow her, as she walked. Her perfect feminine curves refreshed memories of contestants in beauty pageants. She carried herself with pride as her glistening straight hair swayed rhythmically to her catwalk.

'Welcome to our office,' Sim said, as soon as she recovered from her astonishment at the change in the weather and the failure of electricity.

'Thank you. May I know your good name please,' Goonj enquired majestically.

'Sim,' came the reply.

Sim showed her Aanchal's vacant seat. Goonj occupied it with an imposing demeanour and glanced at the opposite seat where Neel sat engrossed in his work. Her eyes rested on him for a moment, as if waiting for him to look up, to strike a conversation.

Then she shifted her gaze to Trisha and said, 'Mr. Cruz informed me that you would introduce me to *D'light D'signz.*'

'Sure,' Trisha said with a subtle smile.

'You will be provided with all the relevant details once you submit all the prerequisites, mainly the details regarding your previous projects. Instantly, Goonj's extravagant smile shrunk, like the skin of a shrivelled fruit, as if she had not expected such a response.

'Oh, the official procedures!' she sighed.

'So, can I get introduced to the team with whom I'm supposed to work?' Goonj asked.

'Yeah sure,' Trisha said.

'Can you spare five minutes, Neel and Jay for a short meeting?' Trisha asked, looking across to their seats.

Jay was on a call. He raised his arm midair as if to say, 'I will just finish this call and be there.'

'I'll join you, as soon as Jay is free,' Neel's immediate response came.

'You have a good rapport with them,' Goonj's words of appreciation rose from her lips, but her eyes somehow failed to express the warmth that her speech conveyed.

Soon, Neel and Jay joined them and settled themselves on either side of Trisha.

Trisha said to her team, 'The sole purpose of this meeting is the introduction of Goonj, who has joined our firm as an intern.'

Then she shifted her attention to Goonj and said, 'Now it's your turn. Go ahead and introduce yourself.'

'Hi! I am Goonj. I'm quite popular among my clients, as a freelance interior designer, but I chose to join Dream Dales, just because I want to work on something more challenging,' Goonj boasted.

'That's great!' Jay said with a wide smile. I am Jay. 3-D designing is my passion and my profession too. Pleased to meet you.'

'Pleasure is all mine,' Goonj replied, flashing an alluring smile.'

'Hi! Neel here. . .'

Before Neel could complete his introduction, Goonj intervened, 'I would be glad if you could help me in brushing up my 3-D designing skills.'

Neel looked at Goonj in astonishment and asked, 'How do you know that I'm a 3-D designer?'

'Oh! That is simple. I saw you working when I entered,' Goonj replied smartly.

Neel exchanged a quick glance with Trisha, maintaining a pleasant expression.

'Yeah, I can help you, though we don't get much spare time here,' Neel replied.

'Jay is the master of the art. He would be the right person to approach,' Neel added, with a glitter in his eyes.

'Sure, I can help you in every possible way,' Jay said sportively.

'Thank you for your willingness to support,' Goonj said, with an icy expression in her eyes, passing a quick glance on all of them.

'We can disperse now,' Trisha concluded.

At lunchtime Goonj asked Sim, 'Is the cafeteria functioning?'

'Yes, very much,' Sim replied.

Soon, Goonj left for the cafeteria.

Trisha had taken a half day leave as she had some plans for the rest of the day.

'Is there any problem?' Neel asked, following her to the corridor, as she walked out of the office.

'What's your opinion about Goonj?' Trisha asked Neel.

'It's too early to comment,' Neel replied.

'Where are you going?' he asked.

'To the temple, I need to find a solution to something that's been bothering me,' Trisha replied gravely.

'I'll come with you,' Neel said.

'Yeah! You reach the temple. I'll send the location,' Trisha said.

CHAPTER SEVEN

Trisha reached home, took a bath, and headed towards Krishna temple to seek the blessings of the Lord, the supernatural Guru as well as Maharshi Trikaldarshi, whom she had accepted as her earthly Guru, before she took her first step in the task entrusted to her. She knew the Will-o'-Wish was the most powerful weapon in the world with intuitive powers, but a spiritual Guru's guidance and blessings could turn the tables in the toughest of battles.

When Trisha reached the temple, the evening *pooja*, the routine sacred ritual of the temple to please the Lord, was yet to begin.

Walking a few steps from the entrance, she saw a *rishi*, carrying the sacred water of the Ganga in an earthen pot for the upcoming pooja. He was clad in a white cotton dhoti with a long piece of the same fabric draped around his shoulders, its ends hanging down loosely, covering the front part of his body. His long black hair was tied up in a bun on top of his head.

She approached the rishi and said, 'Namaste, I must meet the Maharshi urgently.'

'The revered Maharshi isinChandrashala.'

She bowed and took leave from the rishi. Thenproceeded to the hall of learning where she saw the Maharshi in meditation.

Neel was already waiting there, seated on a straw mat. He had found his way to Chandrashala with the guidance of Gurumata Ritambhara Devi. Trisha observed that a few more rolled up mats rested against the wall. She picked one, spread it out, and sat down in Padmasana, the yogic lotus pose,waiting for the Maharshi to come out of his meditation. Soon the venerable sage opened his eyes and beckoned her to come over.

Trisha walked towards him and bowed.

Maharshi Trikaldarshi said, 'I will try to answer all the baffling questions which besiege your senses.

Goonj, the powerful black magician is in your close quarters. She wields the power of evil forces to reign over the underworld. She has landed here, not by chance. It is a part of a conspiracy by some anti- national forces. It is part of a planned attack on the youth of the nation. She has accepted a lump sum amount in advance with a promise to cater to theiranti-social activities. She is the topmost supplier of drugs and alcoholic beverages, and a prime link in the chain of human trafficking.

She leads the youth of the nation astray by attracting them to porn content through pop up advertisements. Gradually their attention is pulled towards physical pleasures, and the youngsters get trapped in unethical activities beyond their age, leaving behind educational quests. Further, they fall prey to pre-arranged virtual and physical meetings with strangers who introduce them to drugs and intoxication. The victims accept it as a cool lifestyle, either to celebrate special occasions or to get relief from setbacks in life.

Aanchal is her mosttrusted aide. Goonj knows that your firm would soon play a major role in designing the interiors of massive colleges across India. Aanchal joined your firm as per Goonj's instructions, so that she could influence the lives of as many youths as possible.

The Guru's words confirmed the strong intuitions that surfaced in her mind about the reality behind the sudden appearance of Goonj. The extra-sensory crystal, the Will-o'-Wish gave her the power to perceive the extremely dangerous vibes of Goonj. Trisha could also visualise a scary future, if Goonj's evil plans materialise.

The Maharshi continued, 'Drugs and alcohol, trap brilliant minds, disabling their senses from recognizing the difference between good and evil.

The merits acquired by your selfless soul in all your past births is the highest in this world, so the Lord has chosen you as the reigning wielder of the invincible Will-o'-Wish.'

'The presence of the Will-o'-Wish creates a powerful aura which nullifies all evil influences on its possessor. Goonj's black magic can never trace the Will-o'-Wish or its possessor.'

'Goonj must be stopped now! Take charge and destroy her chain which is active across the country! Save the innocent people!' the Maharshi commanded.

Trisha bowed before the Maharshi, and vowed, 'I will seal the fate of Goonj! She will never rise again to play with the lives of the people!'

'May God bless you,' the Maharshi said, and he walked out of Chandrashala for the evening pooja.

Thus, the meeting with the Guru culminated, lighting Trisha's path for an undercover investigation against her villainous opponent who was accomplished in the art of silent attacks, using the powers of the invisibles.

CHAPTER EIGHT

Trisha walked towards Neel, who was waiting patiently for herin Chandrashala and said, 'The Maharshi has warned that Goonj is a black magician and a threat to society. It is necessary to curb her activities.'

'So, the matter is much more serious than I thought,' Neel said with a sigh.

'We must immediately visit the buildings designed by her,' Trisha said.

'What will we do there?' Neel asked.

'We must meet the residents of the area to find out if they are well off,' Trisha said with a serious expression in her eyes.

'First, we need to find the location of her previous projects. Let me check the office mail. Goonj must have mailed it,' Neel said.

'No, she hasn't,' he continued.

'I knew she would not. Let's check her website. She surely needs a website for freelance designing,' Trisha said, striking her right fist hard on her left palm.

'Yes, you are right. Two of the buildings designed by her are in and around our city,' Neel confirmed, after checking Goonj's website. 'The nearest one is The Grand Villa Complex in Dhoomketu Lane.'

'Let's not waste any time; we must get there fast,' Trisha said.

At the entrance of The Grand Villa, they saw a car which was about to enter the complex gate. The car stopped, and two people emerged from it. One of them was a young lady who was sobbing uncontrollably. An elderly man who accompanied her was trying to console her.

A few people were standing under the shade of a huge tree. Some of them were young while others were elderly people. Trisha walked up to them.

'Hi,' Trisha said to them.

'Hello,' they responded.

'Why is the lady weeping?' Trisha asked.

'Yesterday, her son who was my daughter's classmate, went missing,' replied one of the ladies.

'He used to be a brilliant student until he and his family members shifted to The Grand Villa. Almost every house in this complex has a sad story to narrate,' an old lady who stood next to her added.

'Are you waiting for someone?' Trisha asked them.

'Yes, we are waiting for our children. The school bus will arrive soon,' came the reply from a lady who was one among the gathering.

'We are conducting a survey on the health and wellness of the students living in this locality. We are interviewing the public to understand the issues faced by the youth and identify its root cause. Your cooperation would help us to find a solution to these problems. Could you please spare some time for an interview?' Trisha requested.

One of the ladies wearing a peacock blue kurta with a combination of sea green slim fit bottom said, 'We are all anxious about the health of our children. We are ready for the interview.'

Neel adjusted his camera to shoot the interview. The lady continued, 'The school going children and college students in our area are facing serious health issues. One of the girls living in The Grand Villa had recently gone for a picnic with her college mates but when she returned, she had lost her mental balance, and now she is undergoing psychiatric treatment. Nobody knows what happened to her.'

A gentleman who stood just behind her nodded in agreement and said, 'Another student, a boy of eighteen, faced traumatic conditions because of drug addiction. He is now undergoing recovery treatment.'

'Another youngster, an alcoholic, attacked his mother for not giving him enough pocket money,' an elderly lady added.

'We long for the simple joys of life, but of late, the peace of our locality is lost, due to a boisterous gang of college students in our area. Their favourite pastime is to gather at the darkest corners of the street after sunset. Sometimes they fight and then, it gets so scary that once the police had to intervene,' one of the parents added.

'Every morning, we find empty broken beverage bottles strewn here and there,' another parent said.

'Thank you for bringing out the real issues of your locality. We will do the needful to get the attention of the authorities and soon find a solution to your problems. Trust us, everything will be all right soon,' Trisha reassured them.

Neel nodded, his eyes beaming with hope, he said, 'We will make sure, happy days are not far off. With this assurance, they took leave of them.

Just then a school bus arrived, and a few students who seemed to be in their teens,got down from it. The girls were wearing white shirts and red and black chequered tunics. They wore their hair in ponytails. The boys were dressed in white shirts and beige toned pants.The reunion of the students with their guardians was a happy sight.

'Tomorrow morning, our destination will be Goonj's residence. We must search her house for evidence regarding her involvement in the miseries of these people,' Trisha said to Neel as they walked towards their vehicles.

'Do you think it would be easy to enter her house?' Neel asked.

'No, but we can't let Goonj continue with her wicked and atrocious activities,' Trisha said firmly.

Next morning, as planned, Trisha and Neel set out on their bikes towards Goonj's residence. From the main street, Trisha turned left to the pocket road under the guidance of the Will-o'-Wish. Neel followed her on his bike. The narrow road, which led them to their destination, was flanked by teak trees. They kept riding for a while, before they reached a dead end, where they halted facing a large compound.

High rising walls with a sturdy, towering gate was all that met their eyes. It was impossible for anyone to even peep into the compound that lay beyond. The gate was not locked, at least the lock was not visible.

Suddenly, Trisha saw some alphabets drifting in the air. She could make out that they were made of ultraviolet rays, invisible to the naked eyes. The dancing letters quickly reordered themselves – revealing a spell.

'Access Storm Weaver!' Trisha uttered twice to herself, and a hidden alley appeared through the centre of the gate.

'Oh, the gate was just ornamental! What magic did you use?' Neel asked with surprise evident in his eyes.

'How will it remain magic, if I tell you?' Trisha asked jovially.

Stepping inside the arched entrance – they started walking through the alley, flanked by beautiful dangling vines. The magical letters followed them and this time, rearranged themselves in the reverse order.

'Weaver Storm Access!'

The spell had its effectas soon as Trisha uttered them, and the passage closed – as if it never existed.

In the middle of a sprawling lawn, stood a huge, seemingly roofless villa, challenging the clouds to reach the sky higher than eyes could trace. The villa was decked with decorative plants – loaded with bunches of lavender flowers. A pathway paved with red stones led to the entrance of the villa.

Suddenly Trisha said, 'Don't walk on the red stones in the pavement; magical hands will clasp you, if you do.'

Neel looked at her in astonishment but without voicing his queries, he said, 'I'll be right behind you.'

Immediately, the pathway started glowing with intermittent fluorescent green stones, alternating with the red ones. Trisha hopped on to the first brightly lit fluorescent stone.

'It's safe towalk on the fluorescent stones,' said Trisha as she hopped onto them, one after the other and soon reached the grassy area from where a staircase with seven steps rose.

The stairs led them to the entrance of the mansion. Trisha's enhanced vision showed her a simmering pond beyond the entrance door. It was a death knell for trespassers.

'Stay away from the door; it is a trap! Whoever touches it, would fall into the boiling pond beyond it,' Trisha said, turning towards Neel.

Will-o'-Wish guided Trisha to the pillar adjacent to the door, on which colourful geometrical patterns indicated the actual entry point. Trisha drew the alphabet Z with her index finger inside a black circle, followed by the mirror image of Z. Immediately, the invisible circular door, which looked like a window, opened and they entered.

The interior looked like a well-lit cave with a sparkling chandelier made of deodar cones in the centre. The cave wall facing the entrance was the replica of a hillside blooming with pink dianthus spiked flowers and royal blue delphiniums dancing in the breeze. Their petals shining with water droplets sprinkled on them from the spring trickling down the hillside. It was a marvellous sight. The exquisite sofas that graced the cave looked like snow decorated with cushions, made of soft white fur.

They walked to the left side of the cave where an arched curtain of beaded strings hung from the ceiling. The curtain held multi-coloured bells at the tip of each string. Trisha pulled a string with a red bell at its tip, opening an invisible door, which led to a glass passage. As she tiptoed ahead of Neel, she signalled with a finger on her lips to maintain absolute silence. Neel nodded and followed her. Suddenly they were taken aback, as multiples of their look-alikes stared back at them. They realised that the whole passage was constructed with stylish vertical mirrors, which created numerous mirror images. As they walked ahead, the passage became darker and darker.

Trisha halted and touched the wall. Immediately, it slid open, revealing a smoky chamber. The smoke rose from the smouldering pieces of timber in the centre of the dimly lit space. Neel pointed towards a staff which was suspended in mid-air without support. It had a carved human skull at one of its ends and the other end tapered like a spear. It seemed to be guarding a black shapeless stone which was placed below it with a red star drawn on it. It represented the devil whom Goonj worshipped, to gain powers. A human skull and two bones in criss-cross fashion was placed in front of it. Some red petals were strewn around the stone. Neel clicked a few photos of the strange room. Immediately, the magical staff turned; its sharp, pointed spear-like end, darting towards them, in an attacking mode. Within a split second, they retraced their steps and Trisha closed the chamber. Without uttering a word, they walked all the way back to the cave-hall.

Fragrant fumes rose from a bronze bowl kept towards the far right of the cave. Trisha picked the bowl and placed it under the deodar cone chandelier. As the fumes touched the chandelier, it started sliding towards the right and a fleet of stairs appeared which led to an opening in the ceiling.

'Let's see where it leads us,' Trisha said.

Carefully, they walked upstairs. When they reached the exit in the ceiling, a rare sight welcomed them – they were surrounded by clouds all around – some of them appeared as if they were soft bunches of cotton, while others swayed like rising fumes. What caught their fancy was a swing which seemed to hang from nowhere.

'Goonj uses it for her recreation,' Trisha said.

They walked further into the enigmatic space. When Trisha touched one of the clouds, it became transparent revealing Goonj's secret locker. It was locked using a sound wave. Trisha tapped her fingers on her left palm – creating a sound that unlocked the safe, revealing bundles of notes stacked one over the other. Neel clicked photographs of her hidden wealth which she had amassed, unlawfully.

Next to the locker was a huge screen. She typed a secret password in the air, opening a folder that contained a video.It was a recording of Goonj's meetings with the head of the anti-social organisation with whom she had illegal financial dealings. Another folder gave access to the data regarding her dealings in drugs, alcohol, and human trafficking. It also listed the contact details and photographs of the members of the gang involved in it.

'This evidence will NAIL her . . .' Trisha said triumphantly.

'. . . and her partners too!' Neel joined in with a jubilant thumbs up.

They were content with the evidence of the nefarious activities of Goonj.Neel collected all the data necessary to proveGoonj's criminal record.Without wasting much time,they found the safest way out, from Goonj's abode.

Their next destination was the newsroom of *Jaago – The Awakening* channel to warn the public about the vicious activities of Goonj, at the earliest. On reaching the office of *Jaago*, they contacted Neel's friend, Ryan, the Managing Director of the channel and shared all the evidence against Goonj with him. Immediately, he agreed to relay the sensational news in the upcoming news broadcast.

On their way back home, Trisha called up her boss, Mr. Cruz to inform him about the recent developments. Sensing the gravity of the situation, he decided to dismiss Goonj to save the image of his firm.

CHAPTER NINE

Trisha reached home by the evening when the breaking news of the arrest of Goonj, themain accused of a silent attack on the nation, flashed across the television screen.

'Look there, Trisha, you are making waves since afternoon!' Swish said with excitement. Jaago News captivated the attention of her parents too, as it hailed Trisha and Neel for Goonj's arrest.

The broadcaster read, 'Goonj, the proprietor of Jhilmil Interiors, under arrest. Her connections with the drug nexus – EXPOSED! The authorities arrested Goonj, based on complaints received against her, regarding her involvement in drug trafficking and ample evidence collected from Goonj's residence by two young sleuths – Trisha and Neel.'

The evidence of her crime: the video of her drug dealings with international drug smugglers followed by Trisha's interview with the residents, along with the photographs of Goonj'ssecret chamber, where she practised witchcraft, were simultaneously relayed.

The news continued, 'The interview of the residents of The Grand Villa Complex reveals the despair of her victims. The outlandish crime of captivating the minds of innocent youngsters, using witchcraft, has invited public wrath. Now, the law of the land will prevail, and its verdict on this peculiar tale will be final.'

'Goonj deserves punishment for her heinous acts. I am proud of you for saving our nation, from an imminent self-destruction,' her father said, patting her with beaming eyes.

'You took a bold decision. Stay strong!' her mother added, her iron will, evident in her expression.

'Trisha, I am with you too,' Swish said with a smile.

Just then, they heard some voices outside.

Swish parted the window curtains and looking outside, she said, 'There is someone at the gate.'

Trisha went out to meet the youngsters who had gathered in front of her residence.

A tall boy came forward and said, 'Hi!'

'Hello!' Trisha said pleasantly, though she had never met him before.

He continued, 'I am Yash, an engineering student. We are the residents of Dhoomketu Lane.'

Another boy of the same age group, who stood next to him said, '. . . and I'm Rajat. We are members of the Vigilant Youth Organisation. We have called for a Human Chain Campaign against Goonj, her enterprise, Jhilmil Interiors, and all those who were part of the racket, in Victor Stadium tomorrow, demanding the most rigorous punishment for them.'

'Our nation needs alert and active youth organisations like yours. Keep doing good work!' Trisha said.

'It was all because of you that the nation woke from oblivion,' Yash said with true regard in his tone.

He added, 'Her victims all over the nation have started connecting with us as soon as we announced the Human Chain Campaign.'

'Multiple cases have been registered against her across the nation. You have shown the world, the true colours of the demoniac Goonj. You are truly awesome!' said Rajat, his voice ringing with appreciation.

Trisha said warmly, 'I feel it was my duty to act instantly and spread awareness about such anti-national activities, before it was too late.

She recollected the series of adventures that unfolded, earlier that day, leading to the arrest of Goonj. After handing over a copy of the evidence against Goonj at the office of Jaago News, Trisha had contacted the President of the Vigilant Youth Organisation, Meghraj, who had arranged an urgent meeting with a few members of the group at their office near The Grand Villa. By then, the news of Goonj's infamous involvement in the narcotics trade, as well as the fact that she was a black magician had already been relayed. This shocking revelation was enough to trigger the wrath of the residents of the locality. Trisha, Neel and the Vigilant Youth activists took up the responsibility of supporting the close relatives of the victims. A few of them proceeded to the local police station to lodge their complaints. Trisha and Neel accompanied them.

Mr. Cruz terminated Goonj from her position without notice, immediately, after receiving Trisha's call. She left for home soon after the incident. At that very instant, the Will-o'-Wish discharged her mobile phone's battery. This disconnected her from her accomplices at the crucial hour when the news about her involvement in the crime was being relayed.

Once she entered the premises of her villa, the Will-o'-Wish locked her inside her car, making it impossible for her to escape. She was completely out of her wits and unaware of the fact that a non-bailable arrest warrant had been issued against her. Finally, she was nabbed by the police, who were not far behind her, accompanied by

Trisha and Neel. The overpowering influence of the Will-o'-Wish sucked the powers of Goonj, making it easier for the police to access the onsite evidence against her.

'Trisha, can we have a photograph with you?' the students requested, bringing Trisha back from her trail of reminiscences.

'Sure,' Trisha agreed, and a snap was clicked. The photograph became viral.

Sleep evaded Trisha, as messages and posts on social media kept pouring in. Many wanted to get first-hand information from her.

That night, it was not long before she fell asleep, when she had another dream. A sharp ultraviolet beam of light laden with tears hit Neel, right in his heart.

She could visualise Goonj, laughing devilishly. Alarmed, she woke up. She saw the Will-o'-Wish glowing with a bright crimson light on her palm. Sensing danger, she switched on the light.

'Is Neel going to be the victim of her vengeance?' 'Why has your smile lost its sheen today?' she asked the glowing statue of Krishna.

'Please show a way out of this danger.'

Immediately, the Will-o'-Wish changed its colour, and it started glittering with a blue hue which indicated that the Lord would guide her through the bleak hour. This indication was enough for her to ace up for a brave fight, against all odds.

That morning, she got ready for the office early. She intended to reach there even before the attendant arrived.

Trisha said to her mother, 'I can't wait for the breakfast, as something urgent has come up.'

'Breakfast is ready, I'll pack it for you,' her mother said with all earnestness. That is how her mother always was, sweet and caring.Trisha took her tiffin, smiled at her mother, and rushed out saying aloud, 'Thank you ma.'

She drove off without delay and soon, found herself fleeting upstairs to her office. As the door opened, she saw Neel seated on his chair. He was about to drink water. The Will-o'-Wish warned her that the water in the bottle was under a spell.

She moved like lightning, screaming, 'Neel, Nooo!'

Startled, Neel shifted the bottle away from his mouth.

'Don't swallow even a drop of that water. Spit it off, please!!' Trisha cried in one breath.

'Give the bottle to me. I will drain it.'

Astonished, Neel kept the bottle aside and walked off towards the sink near the stockroom, adjacent to their office.

'Did you drink the water?' Trisha asked.

'No, I didn't. Though a drop fell into my mouth, I washed it off,' Neel replied.

Trisha heaved a sigh of relief and sat down on the couch near the door. Neel sat next to her and asked softly, 'Why do you look so agitated?'

'I'll clear the food in the fridge and drain all the water bottles,' Trisha said, rising from her seat.

As she was about to move away, Neel held her hand, and turned her around, to face him. Then he asked, 'Will you tell me, what is troubling you? Is it Goonj again?'

'Yes, Goonj has used the *Water Spell*! Misfortune will befall the person on whom the spell has been targeted,' Trisha replied, raising her moist eyes towards him.

Without wasting a moment, she rushed to the sink followed by Neel.

'I will clear all the bottles myself. Keep away! Don't let the water fall on you,' she said, continuing with the task single handedly.

But Trisha's mind was not at peace, as the Will-o'-Wish still glowed crimson. She turned around and glanced at Neel. She could see dark clouds around him. She was sure that the droplet of water that he had ingested had started showing its effect.

She knew it was impossible to nullify the effect of the spell, once it found its mark. He would have to suffer the inevitable pain, yet a strong belief in her heart voiced that no misfortune would ever bog him down. Neel would surely emerge victorious, wading through the dark hours with courage, holding on to the string of hope.

CHAPTER TEN

'Baby Doll, we are thinking of your marriage,' dad said that evening, when she reached back home. A nice proposal has come for you. The boy owns a garment export company. He is coming to see you tomorrow.

'But dad, I don't want to get married now, especially to someone whom I have never met or known before,' Trisha said.

'You are already twenty-two, we cannot wait any longer. As per your horoscope, you must get married this year as it is the most auspicious time for you to tie the nuptial knot.'

'If you don't get married this year, your marriage will get delayed for the next ten years,' her mom said, holding Trisha's horoscope in her hand.

Trisha remembered, once a fortune teller had warned her, 'If you marry against your father's wishes, it will have a grave impact on his health.'

She loved her father dearly and could not even imagine being the cause of his pain.

'Next year, I will retire, so I wish to see you settled as early as possible,' dad added.

The next morning was a Sunday. Trisha's mother expected that she would wear a saree that day, when the boy and his parents came to see her, as per the tradition of arranged marriage. She chose to wear a salwar suitinstead, for two main reasons: the first being the comfort of the attire and the second and the most prominent reason was her disinterest in the whole idea of dressing up as an exhibit for an unknown family, whom she was not keen on meeting. In her heart of hearts, she prayed that they would reject her.

When the guests arrived, Trisha went to meet them with tea and snacks. She bowed and said namaste.

They reciprocated her greeting warmly. She was aghast when her father introduced her to the prospective groom, Dheer, and his mother. The reason was that as per his biodata he was just three years older than her, but in person he seemed to be well above forty.

The 'boy' smiled and fixed his gaze on her which made Trisha uncomfortable.

A lean man of middle stature came in at that moment. Trisha was happy that Dheer's attention shifted to the newcomer. The lady introduced the gentleman as Dheer's father, Mr. Shalva.

'Namaste,' Trisha greeted him with joined palms, welcoming him with a smile.

He seemed preoccupied in his conversation with Trisha's father, 'My legs had a tingling feeling after the long and tiring journey. Your lawn is spacious. A stroll out there has made me feel better.'

He settled himself on the sofa and Trisha offered him tea, which he accepted pleasantly.

'Did you talk to each other?' Mr. Shalva asked, shifting his glance from his son to Trisha.

'No, they have not. I was about to suggest the same so that they know each other better,' Mrs. Shalva replied with a smile. All family members agreed.

Trisha followed Dheer into the lawn, when her eyes met Swish's, who raised her eyebrows as if she were asking

Trisha's opinion. As they walked past her, Swish held her hand and squeezed it warmly. Trisha responded with a thoughtful but calm nod.

'It has been two years since I began my garment industry. Generally, I keep very busy with my work. I would like to know, what kind of life partner you wish for?' Dheer asked, once they were in the lawn.

'One who would be understanding, loving and caring,' she replied.

'Our family is well known in Bengaluru, as we have been living there for the past thirty years. My father is a real estate businessman but as he is unwell, he does not go out much these days. We are a family of four. My younger sister is in college now. She could not accompany us, as she was preparing for her exams. Usually, women in our family do not go out to work. After marriage you can be a homemaker and enjoy your time with my parents at home, as I may have to travel for business requirements,' he continued.

I have not yet decided about marriage, Trisha thought, as Dheer was nowhere near the man of her dreams. Neither did his visualisation about his future partner impress her nor did his personality. Moreover, she wanted to do something noble for the society and that would require her to interact with the common people.

'Would you like to say something?' he asked.

'I am more of an independent person. I am an interior designer, and I love my work. I do not think I can ever settle as a homebird.'

After their little private talk, she made up her mind to reject the proposal.

Suddenly, it started raining and both ran inside for cover. Trisha was happy as she did not wish to continue the conversation.

Soon, the guests departed. Her father told them that he would discuss with his daughter and convey their decision later.

They had a family meeting soon, to discuss the proposal. Dad said, 'They were ready to fix the marriage immediately, but I thought it better to check with my friend in Bengaluru about their family before we take a final decision.'

Trisha said, 'Dheer's idea of marriage is quite different from mine. His family is very conservative. He prefers a homemaker, but I am rather an outdoor person. I told him so, frankly,' trying to convince her parents to drop the proposal.

Her dad said, 'Your worldly knowledge is limited regarding the pains that one has to go through to attain a respectable position in society. The young man is well-settled, with his own business at such an early age. He works hard and takes care of his family. These days, it is difficult to find such responsible young men.'

Finally, her mother said, 'We should check if their horoscopes match, too.'

That evening Trisha rang up Neel.

'I have something important to tell you, Neel,' she said.

She chose to share her emotional turmoil with him as he was the only one, whom she could think of, who would, not only understand her but also lighten her feelings of uneasiness.

'Yes, Trisha, your voice is breaking. Here the network is low as it is raining heavily,' Neel said, walking out from the hospital room, where his cousin who was suffering from typhoid, was admitted.

'I cannot hear you clearly. It is thundering now. I will call back when the weather is clear,' Neel added.

'But it is . . .' before Trisha could finish, the call was disconnected. In utter desperation she went back to her bed, trying to figure out a way that would free her from the dilemma, she was in – whether to accept the advice of her parents or go by her heart and say an outright no to the proposal.

In her restlessness, she turned to the statue of Krishna and asked, 'I cannot even imagine the thought of marrying Dheer. What should I do?'

'Please, help me to take the right decision.'

The Lord's countenance glowed with a mysterious smile. He seemed to have other plans for her.

CHAPTER ELEVEN

The next day Trisha reached office, earlier than usual. Neel was already there. The moment her eyes fell on Neel, the tears which she had held back till then, started rolling down her cheeks. He took a stride forward, just in time, to catch the teardrops in his palm and said, 'They are precious, never let them fall.'

Then, he held her hand in his and asked earnestly, 'Will you tell me what happened?'

'Yesterday, a family visited us. It was not a casual visit. Mrs. and Mr. Shalva came to ask my hand in marriage for their son, Dheer. Their intention was to fix the marriage, immediately. My parents also want me to get married at the earliest, as they think it is my good luck that I got such a perfect match. He is a garment exporter, the boy, I mean.' Trisha paused, as Neel stepped back with widened eyes and an expression of shock spreading across his face. His raised eyebrows created lines of anxiety, stretching from one end of his forehead to the other.

'Trisha,if you don't like him, you should firmly say – NO. Nobody can force you to marry someone whom you don't like,' he said.

'Each time I rejected a proposal, my parents stood by me, as they believed that I deserved a better match. But now, they feel that Dheer is the best life partner for me. They are not ready to hear anything against this proposal.'

'My father has shielded us from all cares, till now. We are his treasure. He is the best dad in this world.'

Trisha sat on her chair with tears swelling in her eyes.

Neel took a chair and sat next to her. He pressed her palm softly and said, 'Stop crying and listen to me.'

Neel's soothing touch calmed her a bit.

'What's your opinion about me? Do you think I will be a good life partner for you?' Neel asked, raising her chin.

Trisha stopped sobbing suddenly, and asked, 'Are you serious? What about Netra? Aren't you in love with her? Are you saying all this out of sympathy?' Trisha looked puzzled, as she blurted out questions after questions.

'Sympathy! By no means! You don't know what you mean to me,' he paused, as a sea of emotions surfaced on his face.

'Netra does not even exist in my remotest thoughts. From the time we met, I liked you. As our friendship grew, I started yearning for your presence and company, day after day. I felt, as if, an unseen thread pulled me towards you,' said Neel, unleashing his bottled-up emotions.

Trisha could not take her eyes off Neel, as if she were in a daze. Then she managed to ask in a subdued voice. 'Is this all true? If so, why didn't you ever ...?' she sighed.

'Yes, true and from the bottom of my heart. Don't you like me too? Tell me honestly,' Neel urged, searching for truth in her eyes.

'Yes, I do.' she said, her melting eyes meeting his intense gaze. Then she gradually lowered her eyes.

'Look at me. How long have I wished to hear those sweet words! Say them again,' Neel said, holding her face in his palm.

'I like you..., I always did,' Trisha replied softly.

'How pure and how beautiful, you look,' Neel whispered.

'Once I complete my higher studies, I plan to start my own business. It is just a matter of two more years. You will reign as the princess of my heart,' Neel said earnestly.

Trisha's searching eyes lingered on his expressive countenance for a while. She could sense nothing but truth in those sincere eyes.

'You always make me feel so special. I would have considered myself to be the luckiest, if you were my life partner,' Trisha's voice rose from her soul.

'But time . . .! My father will retire next year, so he wants both his girls to get married as early as possible. Moreover, my parents are not ready to wait any longer as my horoscope says I must get married this year or wait for ten more years,' Trisha said with a sigh, tears brimming on her eyelashes. The radiance of her face faded as clouds of despair started setting in, as the realisation of the trouble that she was in, started clawing and her emotions bled.

'As per my parents, being well settled in life is the most important criteria for a groom. You are planning to pursue higher education. If I introduce you to my parents and tell them that we wish to get married, do you think they would agree? So, how will we convince them? What can we do?'

'We will not run away from home. It would be like hauling burning coal into the well-meaning hearts of our parents. They keep us in their prayers always. We grew up in the shade of their blessings. Such a step would not only pain them but also tarnish our families' image,' Neel gravely analysed the situation that they were in.

'Yes, I shudder at the thought of how my dear dad and mom would face the world,if my actions surpassed their wishes and caused them indelible pain.Wouldn't it affect the marriage prospects of Swish too?'

'But I can't live without you!' Neel held her hand and broke down.

'Neel, I feel trapped in the clutches of this terrible fate. Pardon me for being the cause of your pain,' Trisha sobbed.

'No, do not blame yourself! I cannot see you crying,' Neel said, wiping Trisha's tears, trying hard to fight back the fresh tear drops that rolled down his cheeks, which seemed to obey his heart, overruling the command of his intellect.

She too, did not know how to pacify him. Words seemed powerless.

That day marked the end of their love story . . . a love story which they tried to bury in their hearts forever, such that, it would never see sunlight.

Soon preparations for Trisha's marriage began; on the other hand, pangs of separation took a heavy toll on Neel. It tore him apart. He tried to find solace in stringing his heart-wrenching pain into musical compositions which became the soul of his album "The Voice of My Heart." It was released on the day of her wedding. His tearful verses and his soulful voice left an unforgettable mark, deep down the hearts of millions, gripping their senses to the extent that their lips kept humming it gently. It was so infectious that it passed on from listener to listener, who happened to hear his songs – even once.

The Voice of My Heart

Memories . . .

Lying deep in my heart,

Keep searching for you everywhere,

Till pinching reality says,

You are away, too far away.

Won't you come back to me?

My love calls you,
Day and night.
Memories . . .
Walking miles, with your memories,
Hoping to see you somewhere,
Longing for a glimpse of you.
Won't you come back still?
As a shower on my burning heart,
That yearns for you
Day and night.
Memories . . .
Holding on to memories . . .
Waiting for the summer
To light a fire in your heart,
Holding on to hope
That your words would come true,
That once said you are mine.
Let it be forever.
Memories . . .
I will wrap my memories,
And shield them from the world.
My love, lying deep in my soul,
Will rise from the ashes,
Long after I am gone, like a breeze . . .
That keeps blowing,
Day and night.
Memories . . .
Crave to call back the spring,
When we walked together,
Smiling, on the brazen path,
Love floating in the air.
Reminding you, of those days,
And sing along the song of joy,

As we did, forever and ever.

Time seemed to pass at a very slow pace for Neel. Every single minute seemed like a millennium of despair and anguish. The sun never rose without a thought of Trisha, and his eyes could never welcome sleep without dreaming of her.

CHAPTER TWELVE

Three months later.

One fine morning, Neel's phone rang.

'Can you pick me from the airport at 6 AM tomorrow?' the sweet voice echoed in his ear, long after the call ended. The voice at the other end was the one he yearned to hear but could not believe his ears, so he checked the number again. It was a new number, but unmistakably it was Trisha. He was elated at the very idea of meeting her again. Next day, he left home early and rushed to the airport, as it would take nearly an hour to reach there.

When he finally met her, he found her prettier than before. She flashed an electric smile, which came from the depth of her heart. An equally heart-warming smile rose from his lips, which resembled the smile of an innocent child, who had found something precious and long lost. Without uttering a word, he took the luggage from her hand and led her to the car, parked in the waiting area.

'How are you?' he asked as he held the car door open for her.

'I missed you,' came the reply.

'I missed you too,' Neel whispered.

Once she settled herself in the front seat, he kept her luggage in the boot. He drove at a comfortable speed and soon they were on the highway.

'Congratulations on the success of "The Voice of My Heart." Beautiful and heart-touching . . .'

'So, it found its mark,' Neel said, trying hard to hide the agony in his voice but betrayed by a tear glimmering in his eyes.

Trisha's observant eyes caught the pain that he tried to suppress. 'I am sorry,' she said, wishing if she could take back the words she had just spoken.

'Now tell me everything,' he continued, glancing at her, and studying her expression for a fleeting second. His intention was to distract her attention from his pain, as he was curious to hear her part of the story.

'On the day of our wedding, Dheer returned after partying with his friends,completely drunk and started boasting about his achievements in life. I could not take it for too long. I told him that I possess the power to read minds. He was suddenly curious. He asked me if I could reveal what was on his mind. When I said, he drank not to celebrate but to bid farewell to his dreams. He was dumbfounded. I could see a teardrop brimming on his eyelashes, as he retraced his steps. From that day, he kept a safe distance from me. I guessed, it was to safeguard a secret which kept surging in his heart like a wave,' Trisha said.

'I kept waiting for the day when Dheer would open up, but the truth took a winding path to reach me.'

Trisha continued, 'One day, his personal assistant, Ms. Serin, called and expressed her desire to meet me in person. Soon, we met at a restaurant, and she disclosed that Dheer had promised to marry her but had backed out, due to his parents' opposition.'

Neel looked at her with surprise evident in his eyes.

'When I discussed the matter with him, he confessed that he was truly in love with Ms. Serin and that his parents had rejected her, as she belonged to a family which was much below their status.'

'That's how their search finally ended on me.'

Trisha went on, 'I was happy that he had unravelled the truth, later than never. I pondered over the question, whether to stay on in a loveless and meaningless marriage, just for the sake of our parents or separate, so that both of us can lead a more fulfilling life. Finally, Dheer and I decided to part... mutually. I informed my parents about the situation. They were shocked, and couldn't help feeling sorry for arranging my marriage, in such a haste. They advised me to take a stand which would keep me happy.'

There was silence for a moment.

'Love is universal, everyone falls in love at some point of time or the other, but few are lucky enough to remain in love forever. Love that stands the test of time is true love!' Neel said, glancing at her with a maturity that could have been born only from the firsthand experience of the evasive emotion.

Trisha nodded and continued, 'Goonj took her revenge. She couldn't harm me directly, so she targeted you,' Trisha said.

'All is well that ends well! Now we are back to square one,' Neel paused and looked at her.

'You need a change of mood. An outing would help. Don't you think so? Let's go for a long drive. Sim, Jay, and I had planned an outing to the waterfall, in the outskirts of the city. Wouldn't you join us?'

'Sure, I truly miss those wonderful days when we were together,' Trisha replied with a glimmer in her eyes.

Neel steered his car to a halt, as they had reached Cherry Avenue, the spot, which had been fixed as the starting point for their trip. Trisha and Neel stepped out of their car, only to be pleasantly welcomed by a shower of cherry blossoms, carried by a light breeze.

'What a splash of pink!' Trisha said, enchanted by the spectacular view.

'Splendid!' Neel agreed as they revelled in the beauty of spring.

After a while or so, Neel said, 'Sim and Jay are waiting for us in the nearby coffee shop.'

He rang them up. Immediately, they could see their friends, walking towards them.

'Great to see you again!' Trisha greeted them exuberantly.

'Yeah . . . a pleasant surprise indeed!' Sim responded gleefully.

'Yeah . . . I never thought we could meet up so unexpectedly,' Jay said, his expressive eyes spilling joy.

'Hi Dilraj!' Neel said, waving his hand at the man on the wheel of the car which they had hired for the trip.

'Hi!' Dilraj replied, greeting them all with a pleasant smile, as he stepped out of the car. He was a tall young man with a strong build.

'I will be back soon, after parking my car,' Neel said to them, steering his car towards the nearby parking area.

Trisha, Sim, and Jay settled themselves comfortably in the car.

'Didn't Dheer accompany you?' Sim asked.

'My married life with Dheer ended before it started,' Trisha replied, keeping her expressions stable.

'What happened?' Jay enquired with concern.

'We were not made for each other,' Trisha answered with declining spirit as she spoke of her marriage.

Neel rushed back to join others. He was upset when he saw Trisha in a blue mood again. He guessed what could have happened.

'I asked Trisha to join us, so that she could have a change of mood,' Neel said, trying to explain the situation to his friends.

'Come with me,' Neel said to Trisha, and soon they adjusted themselves comfortably on the rear seat. Their journey began.

'Are there any chances of coming across wild animals?' Trisha asked.

'At times snakes and monitor lizards are spotted. It is less likely to come across poisonous snakes, as it is a tourist spot,' said Dilraj.

Neel took Trisha's hand in his and said, 'Your hand is cold.'

'It's just the morning chill,' Trisha replied with a slight smile.

After a while Sim offered snacks and Trisha asked Neel, 'Won't you have some?'

'No, thanks,' Neel shook his head.

'I would like to have some...' Trisha said, shifting her eyes to her hand, which he still held gently.

'Yeah sure!' he nodded, finally releasing her, with a smile.

As they munched popcorn on the way, Trisha caught Neel unawares, watching her fondly from the corner of his eye. Her chocolate brown eyes narrowed, her lips curving into a half smile. He returned a mischievous smile in response before diverting his attention to the scenery outside.

Everyone shared their own funny experiences and when they had nothing personal to recollect, discussions on movies crept in, making their chats lively and vibrant, throughout the length of their journey.

On the way, they saw a Krishna temple and they stopped by to pay a visit. As they walked towards the temple, Trisha noticed two fresh footprints, belonging to an invisible form, that kept leading them towards the interiors of the temple. She passed a quick glance at her companions, but none of them seemed to have noticed the miracle. She felt blessed as she witnessed the vanishing footsteps entering the sanctum sanctorum, where the statue of the smiling Lord resided. She thanked the Lord for protecting her and guiding her through thick and thin, helping her to take the right decisions. Soon, they resumed their journey, their hearts as light as a feather.

After an hour or so, they reached the waterfall which splashed head on, to the rocks beneath, sprinkling water, like a spray of white smoke, all the way down the greenish mountain which finally took the shape of a lustrous stream. The glistening water of the stream, meandering between the sprawling rocks, seemed crystal clear.

'We must be very careful as we walk upon the mossy rocks. They may be slippery,' Sim said.

'Yeah, you are right,' Neel agreed.

'We'll cross the stream,' Jay said as he walked ahead.

'We'll be right behind you,' Sim declared, following him enthusiastically.

Jay and Sim had already crossed the stream halfway, hopping on to boulders that jutted out of the shallow stream.

A cool breeze blew, inviting them to the adventure amidst nature. Neel jumped on to a dry boulder, then extending his hand, said, 'Come on, Trisha! Hold and just take a leap.'

He held her extended palm in a tight grip and pulled her up strongly, helping her to take the leap. She landed safely on the boulder, where Neel stood. She was too close to him now, his left hand encircling her waist. He gazed into her eyes and almost whispered, 'Your eyes hypnotise me. I feel powerless before them.'

She blushed and tried to look away from him.

'Once you asked me why I follow you. I answered you now. Does that satisfy your query?' Neel asked gently.

'What's in your heart?' she asked softly, evading a direct answer, not to feign ignorance towards his feelings for her, but from the longing to hear what lay beneath the intensity of his gaze.

'You... I want you to be with me forever. Like this, hand in hand as each other's better halves, where I will be seen in your eyes and you could be seen in mine; our hearts beating together, as if we were one. Will you marry me?' Neel asked, closely studying her countenance.

She could not believe that her prince charming had just spoken those magical words to her.

'Will you be mine?' he asked earnestly.

She observed every detail of the face which had just revealed its intention and whispered as if in a dream, 'Yes, I will remain yours forever . . .'

His face lit up with boundless joy.

He kissed her forehead gently and she felt completely secure in his arms.

'Shall we cross the stream now?' she asked, her lips blossoming into a smile.

'Oh! the stream...Yeah, we should,' he said, coming back to reality.

'Have you ever spotted lovebirds in the wild?' Jay called out, his finger pointing to a tree. Sim stood next to him, peering through the branches, trying to trace the lovebirds. Trisha and Neel laughed and moved in the direction of their friends.

Once they crossed the stream, they were closer to the waterfall. All of them settled on a huge boulder, on the bank of the stream and watched the beautiful waterfall gushing down from the heights. Jay took out packets of peanuts from his backpack and distributed it to them. Just then a troop of monkeys came out from the wilderness. Trisha threw some peanuts towards them which they grabbed sportively. She had saved a few peanuts beside her, on the rock where she sat, underneath her chunari. A mama monkey with a baby clinging to her belly came close to her and picked her chunari slightly, just enough to grab the hidden peanuts. The funny incident left them rocking with laughter. They had a jovial time together and clicked memorable snaps.

After lunch, they set out on their return journey. Trisha rested her head on Neel's shoulder as he held her close to him. They revelled in the beauty of the winding lush green mountainous route downhill. The weather was calm and so were they. Their life had just settled after an arduous climb uphill. They had tided over the unrest of a stormy night. Sunny days lay ahead, promising happiness, as they had found love, the most precious treasure in the universe.

Glossary

aarti: a traditional Indian way of worship, with lighted lamps and songs in praise of God

choli: a short blouse, worn with lehenga

chunari: a long stole worn by Indian women

dhoti: a long piece of cloth worn by Indian men, draped on the lower part of the body and tucked in front or back of the waistline

floral rangoli: an artistic design using colourful flowers, created on the floor, on festivals

Gurumata: a respectful term for Guru's wife

kadai paneer: a spicy, flavourful Indian cuisine made of cheese

kurta: a long loose-fitting shirt worn in combination with loose fitting pants popularly known as pyjamas

Lucknowi chikankari: a traditional embroidery style from Lucknow, India

lehenga: full ankle length embroidered skirt worn by Indian women on ceremonial occasions

Maharshi: a title given to a sage or teacher who possesses spiritual and mystical knowledge

namaste: an Indian way of greeting with joined palms, which means 'I bow to you'

rishi: a sage

sadhvi: a female ascetic

www.ingramcontent.com/pod-product-compliance
Lightning Source LLC
Chambersburg PA
CBHW031455150726

47990CB00007B/2768